Skylark

Sara Cassidy

orca soundings

ORCA BOOK PUBLISHERS

Library and Archives Canada Cataloguing in Publication

Cassidy, Sara, author
Skylark / Sara Cassidy.
(Orca soundings)

Issued in print and electronic formats.
ISBN 978-1-4598-0591-0 (bound).--ISBN 978-1-4598-0590-3 (pbk.).--
ISBN 978-1-4598-0592-7 (pdf).--ISBN 978-1-4598-0593-4 (epub)

I. Title. II. Series: Orca soundings
PS8555.A7812S49 2014   jc813'.54   C2013-906742-6
                        C2013-906743-4

First published in the United States, 2014
Library of Congress Control Number: 2013954150

Summary: After Angie's father leaves town to find work, her family ends up
evicted and living in their car. Struggling with the realities of homelessness,
Angie discovers slam poetry and her own voice.

*Orca Book Publishers is dedicated to preserving the environment and has
printed this book on Forest Stewardship Council® certified paper.*

Orca Book Publishers gratefully acknowledges the support for its publishing
programs provided by the following agencies: the Government of Canada through
the Canada Book Fund and the Canada Council for the Arts,
and the Province of British Columbia through the BC Arts Council
and the Book Publishing Tax Credit.

Cover image by Dreamstime

ORCA BOOK PUBLISHERS
PO Box 5626, Stn. B
Victoria, BC Canada
V8R 6S4

ORCA BOOK PUBLISHERS
PO Box 468
Custer, WA USA
98240-0468

www.orcabook.com
Printed and bound in Canada.

17 16 15 14 • 4 3 2 1

*For those who
are between homes.*

Prologue

The Spiral Café was a place of move-
ment and color and noise and silence.
The windows would be fogged from our
breathing and from the evening's rain,
which migrated from the damp sweaters
slung on the backs of our chairs.
We spoke intently there. We listened
intently. The air was spiked with words.

"Spiral" was the right name for that café those nights we took our stand at the front of the crowd, adjusted the microphone to the right height—mouth height—and let loose. The words would loop and twirl through the damp air, funnel and *spiral* into waiting ears, banging against eardrums and fueling brains.

All of us would be running on the same fuel, the same drug. Mom says a good story or poem is the only drug. We'd laugh when the story called for it, cry sometimes, hoot and holler "yeah!" We would jump to our feet and cheer when it was done if it had been a good thing, a good trip. If it hadn't been, if it had just been so much talk, if the words hadn't been the right ones to tell the story, we'd clap politely and wait, hopeful for the next performance.

I had my favorite performers. When the MC called their names, I'd settle back into my chair—or I'd lean forward. Ready for something new, something not normal, something that would carry me, nudge me a little to the left or to the right, push me forward or pull me back.

But every time the MC approached the microphone, my heart would drop, too, because one of those times she would call my name, and then it would be up to me to make the words spin and whirl, to give everyone a fine ride, one that would stay with them into the night.

Every Tuesday evening, I would walk through the door of the Spiral Café into that moist, noisy air to find my feet and my voice and let my words tumble out, just the way I'd crafted them, into something whole and sure and living— into something like a home.

Backseat Dreams

That was when we were living in the Buick Skylark, and Mom still managed to look like a million bucks every day. I'd get to school early, sneak through a side door, hustle into a bathroom and wash my hair in freezing water, neck bent hard so I could fit my head under the short tap. I'd have a headache afterward, the water was so cold.

Mom slept across the front seats—every night she laid a small cutting board and a folded towel over the plastic console. Clem and I stretched out in the back, side by side, trading off who would cling to the edge of the seat and who would spend the night squashed against the rough upholstery.

Mom was always neat. She kept her clothes in a small suitcase tucked into the footwell of the front passenger seat. The glove compartment was for toiletries and important documents. My "closet" was a backpack behind the driver's seat, Clem's a sports bag behind the front passenger's. In the outside pockets of our packs we each kept a toothbrush, library card and current two books.

The library was our savior. The librarians never asked questions and answered every one of ours. We'd spend long evenings in the library, moving between the city's seven branches so no one would suspect. Not that there was anything to suspect, Mom would remind us even as we snuck around guiltily. We weren't doing anything wrong, only going somewhere warm, with solid surfaces to do our homework on.

Mom always loved us and looked after us. It wasn't her fault that rent was two grand a month and the waiting time for public housing at least half a year, so we were told. When I tried to fall asleep at night, Clem's bony knee hard in my back, I'd visualize our family name, hand-printed in blue ink—KILPATRICK—inching up a list at the public-housing office, ticking upward to the top spot. Then shining keys lowering from on high. The three of us climbing the last few stairs to a freshly painted door, fumbling with the lock and arguing—the best kind of arguing, the kind you do to pass the time, the kind that is tangy with teasing; *come on, butterfingers! My goodness, Angie, didn't I teach you how to unlock a door?*

I'd drift into sleep with that picture in my head—Mom, Clem and me on the top step, fighting for the keys to our subsidized palace. But the keys always shrunk in my hand, and I'd wake to the rough seat beneath me, my neck crooked against the door, Clem's heavy arm over me. I'd frown into the dark. Lie there in that black soup. Until I heard Mom purring in the front. She refused to let the bare-knuckle hours of our days get in the way of a good sleep. I'd join her in the forgetting place. We always slept well in that car.

Through-Line

Actually, some nights we slept less well in the Buick Skylark. One time, four teenagers rocked the car, and we opened our eyes to their squashed faces at the windows. To them, we must have been like fish in an aquarium—blurry, bleary, unwary, swimming in our sleep. One of them licked the glass. Mom made a move to open her door, and they ran down the street, whooping.

At least they weren't the police, who had rapped on the windshield once or twice, stung our eyes with their flash-lights, told us to move along. But they stopped. Got used to us, got to know Mom and understand that we were neither lazy nor criminal, only unlucky. One cop even dropped things off for us, tucked them under the car if we weren't "home"—a twenty-pack of Timbits, scratchy blankets, pairs of black acrylic socks and, at the start of September, two binders and a five-hundred-sheet pack of loose-leaf paper.

I was embarrassed by my binder. First of all, it matched Clem's—close as we are, that wasn't cool, not when we went to the same school. And the binder felt brutally clean somehow. Righteous. I walked down the hallway my first day back at school and felt like I was marked. Like everyone knew that it wasn't mine, not really.

There was a guy in our old neighborhood who walked with his shoulders heavy, head down, dragging his feet. His old coat was too big, and his dark pants were oil-stained. The shoelaces in his cracked shoes were nothing but brown parcel string. Mom said he slept in the woods of the ravine. One day the guy shuffled past our car wearing a hospital bracelet and holding a plastic bag with big letters announcing *Patient Garment Bag*. He'd been in the hospital, Mom explained, likely for mental health reasons, and when he'd checked out, they had given him his belongings in the big bag. It looked like he was being made a fool of, with that bag. Everyone being told about him. That's how I felt with the binder. As though it glowed and exposed me. *PITY BINDER*, it might say.

At the end of biology class, I asked the teacher if I could use some duct tape—she had rolls of the stuff on top of her filing cabinet. "Sure," she said, hurrying off for lunch, "just close the door behind you when you're done." I covered my binder with that silver-gray tape, then marked it up with a pen—*Angie's Binder*, I wrote, between a thousand Sharpie hearts and stars and even a couple of Saturns with radiating rings. I drew a bird zooming through the cosmos, too, a sweet little bird with a small poof of a crest on its head. I don't know where she came from, that bird. But finally the binder felt like mine. In it, 250 pages of blank loose-leaf paper. Clem got the other 250, and you can imagine that we counted every sheet. It's the perfect thing to do when you're squashed up in the back of a car. That, or play cribbage again.

When things got rough after Dad left, Mom took us to the Single Parent Resource Center. It's an old brick house on a busy street, with nothing around it but gas stations and cheap motels. It's got a bread cupboard—Clem and I nabbed a cheese loaf—a clothing exchange, rooms where you can meet with counselors, and a play area for kids. Clem and I are way too old for the play area—I mean, he's sixteen and I'm fourteen—so we just sat in the waiting area, leafing through Archie comics while Mom talked to the woman at reception. Mom was trying not to cry. She said something like, "How do we stay a family now, without a home and no father? How do we not go flying apart?" The woman answered, "Just keep doing some of the things you always have done. That'll make a through-line. The through-line will carry you."

That evening, we were squished in the car, doing homework by the light of our fancy solar-powered LED lanterns, when Mom said, "Let's head to the Spiral."

When we lived in the apartment with Dad, we'd hit the Spiral Café once a week for hot chocolate. We'd just bundle up after supper, leave the dishes unwashed and walk together, the four of us, down the gray sidewalks, talking and teasing, stealing each other's hats and running, reading lost-cat posters, sizing up new houses. Just being free with each other.

These days, I get anxious whenever Mom suggests spending money. My heart digs in and I say no. But that night, she didn't even give Clem and me time to pretend we didn't want to go. She put the key in the ignition and shifted the gearstick to Drive.

Electrified

I'd never seen the café so busy. A poster on the door announced that it was Slam Night. The chairs were turned toward the front. There was a microphone under a spotlight, and a young guy was giving some kind of speech. He wore pink skinny jeans and a ragged brown sweater. He was talking about people acting cool. He used repetition and rhymes, and he would slow down and speed up his talking depending on what he was saying. He'd draw everyone in with a whisper, then pop them back to reality with a shout. It was somewhere between song lyrics, a poem, a rap, a presidential speech and a televangelist's sermon—it was all of that and none of that. It was mesmerizing.

You put on shades, big-ass shades.
   The windows go black.
You think you're looking out, and
   no one's looking back,
that no one's looking in, at your
   murk and mess and sin.
You try so hard to look so hard, but
   you're soft inside,
like yolk in an egg, you're yellow
   and afraid
that someone's gonna crack you,
   crack you like a safe.
You swagger down the street in your
   combat wear, danger and dare.

*Dogs snap and growl as you
   draw near.
They've got your number, fear's an
   easy cipher.
And you're glad those dogs are
   leashed.
You're glad those dogs aren't free.
That isn't courage.
Look at me. Look into my eyes.
I was brave. I opened my heart.
   I looked in the mirror until its
   silver poured from the frame.
   I stood there, unashamed.
The toughest people have the
   clearest eyes.
The toughest people have the
   clearest eyes.
The toughest people? You see right
   inside.*

The bottoms of my feet tingled. My scalp buzzed. I was electrified. At the end of his piece, the guy went silent, adding to the quiet, but it was too much silence for the air to hold—it burst into applause and whoops. People even stomped their feet.

I turned to Mom and Clem, eyes wide. "Wasn't that the most awesome thing?" But they just smiled weakly and went back to their conversation.

The guy shrugged under the spotlight, then sauntered off the stage. A woman about nineteen years old, twig-thin with bouffed-up black hair and red lipstick, leapt to the mic. "Thank you, Aaron, our reigning slam champion. Aaron's won five weeks in a row. Who's going to knock him out of the ring?" The woman checked a list in her hand. "Violet. It's your chance. You get five minutes to show your stuff."

Violet looked about fifteen. She was dressed simply, in jeans and a sea-green blouse. She had straight brown hair and no makeup. Her poem thing was nothing like Aaron's. She spoke quietly, all in one tone, but her voice beckoned. Everyone leaned forward in their seats, turning their heads slightly to make a straight path between her mouth and their ears. The girl talked about grass-hoppers and loneliness and a field "where mercy grows."

the rain is mauve
the sun is sweet
the dirt is dark and live
the air is a prayer
that you breathe deep
and hold
long
inside
so you don't forget
but you do forget
the field behind the old fire hall
a mile from the 7-Eleven store
where we hang these days
getting hurt and mean and tall

that field behind the old fire hall
where we used to go
where we used to play
    in the weeds where mercy grows

When Violet finished, it was like everyone breathed out at once. The air relaxed. The applause was gentle. I felt dreamy. Violet's poem had opened little rooms in my mind, some that were dark and smelled of dirt, and others that were brightly lit, surgical as a 7-Eleven store.

"Awesome, Violet," Twig Girl said, taking the stage. "And that brings this week's slam to an end. The judges will confer and announce the winner in a jiffy. So, chill for a bit. Get another coffee, talk with your friends. Or start composing your entry for next week's slam. Same time, same place. Sign-up starts at six thirty."

I looked at Mom and Clem. They were in another world. Clem was talking about a BMX competition coming up. Mom nodded along, her eyes a little glazed. It was like she wanted to encourage him but at the same time couldn't, because competitions cost money, and where would that come from? Five minutes later, the judges—two Spiral baristas—took to the stage and announced that Aaron was again the slam champion. He won a can of squid "in natural ink" and a retro penmanship practice book. The prizes were jokey, but Aaron's smile was real. Violet placed third and won a latte.

Back in the car, moving through the city, my thoughts were like chants. Everything I saw was new and urgent and meant more than I'd ever imagined. *Streetlight, autumn night, every drop of rain clearing us of blame. Looking for a place to park, a piece of street for tonight's bedframe. Noah's ark, Skylark, keeping us afloat in the dark…*

The words just kept stringing through my mind. As soon as we parked—in our favorite place, under the big willow on the gravel cul-de-sac behind the Adult Education Center—I opened my binder and wrote until my knuckle was sore and dented from the ballpoint pen.

At midnight, Clem kicked me—hard. "For the last time, turn off your stupid flashlight."

I tucked my binder into my backpack, shut down my flashlight and stared into the black soup, wondering if I'd really be able to step up to the mic, stand under the spotlight and pour out my words the following week at the Spiral Café.

Landlord

What happened was, Mom fell off a ladder when the rung under her feet snapped while she was washing windows at a house in Fairfield. And then she couldn't work because of the pain, but she couldn't get workers' compensation because housecleaners don't have that. We stopped paying the Bruces first, and finally we broke on the rent.

Our landlord was all business, even though we'd lived in that place for seven years and weren't loud or messy. As soon as we were three days late with the rent, a note went up on our apartment door, threatening eviction. Public humiliation, Mom called it, and she scrambled the rent together, scared up an ounce of extra work, borrowed a twenty from a neighbor.

But the following month, we were late again, and *bang,* the note went up, crisp and formal on the dirty door. And the following month. I'd trudge up the stairs after school—Mom didn't let us take the elevator because it was dangerously old—only to be greeted by that stupid white rectangle, a brand, a badge of shame. I learned to rip the page off the door the way Mom did—disdainful, undefeated. Shrug it off, hustle up the money, beat it.

Clem and I would go out in the evenings, pedal our crappy bikes through the city's neighborhoods to rummage Blue Boxes for returnables, stuffing the sticky cans and bottles into the emptied school-bags that swung from our handlebars.

One of those evenings, Clem swiped a gleaming bike from someone's garage and left his own in its place. Did his rounds on that good bike, filling its titanium basket and leather panniers with bottles, ringing its silver bell as he rode down the center line of the city's dark streets. After dumping the night's collection at the apartment, he headed out on his own, telling me not to worry. I thought maybe he was going to sell that bike, but he came home on his old five-speed. He'd returned the rich kid's bicycle and retrieved his own. It wasn't the last time Clem borrowed that kid's bike though. He was always careful with it. Never did a slide or a skid and not one bunny hop.

Mom, meanwhile, scrambled up work with ads on Craigslist and posts on Facebook. She'd weed someone's garden for a few hours or help paint someone's front stairs, but her back would act up and she'd lie on the couch in pain for two days afterward. She applied for jobs too, but pickings were slim, partly because there just weren't a lot of jobs and partly because she had never finished high school.

Finally, she got a job at Sandwich Shack. The owner is nice and lets her sit on a high stool to build sandwiches, which saves her back. He also gives her leftovers for Clem and me. But he won't give Mom more than three shifts a week. Mom says nobody hires full-time because then they'd have to pay for their employees' health insurance and other stuff.

Clem begged to get a job to help out, but Mom gave him the look. The you've-got-homework-to-finish-because-you're-graduating-high-school look.

We couldn't chase the white page away permanently. It kept landing on the door like it was a ghost that wanted in and that was that. Once, I came around the corner after school just as the landlord's teenage son tacked it to the door. I looked at him, hoping that maybe if he was caught in the act, there was some rule that he had to take it down. He smiled, but his lips were tight. He squinted as if he couldn't quite see me. As if I was so small. He left the notice on the door and walked away like he was angry, not saying hello.

I've thought about that notice of his and how it was so mean. Now, I fill my own pages—blue ink on loose leaf. Which is stronger? His scolding legalese? Or these rhymes that find each other with ease?

Gloves

At the BMX track, Clem and I are known as The Kids, but Clem's The Star. The Champ. I like to ride, but mostly I sit on the fence and watch Clem. I gulp when he catches air. My stomach knots when he does his daredevil moves. My eyes hurt following him as he whizzes past—a streak, a blur, a smudge of color. I've heard that the Earth turns fast, spins a thousand miles an hour. Most of the time, that's hard to believe. But not when Clem pumps around the track. Speed is what he is.

Three years ago, the neighborhood association put in the BMX park, along with a basketball court and a community center that has kitchens and meeting rooms but no gym. They put in community gardens too, down the hill from the BMX track. There was a waiting list for the garden plots, but Mom said we weren't good at being on waiting lists. She tried to sound like she was joking, like she was lighthearted.

Mom wandered down to the gardens once when Clem and I were biking. She came back excited. "I've seen community gardens before," she told us, "rich with leaves at this time of year, kale up to your knees, tall garlic stems, peas winding upward—but these garden beds? Nothing. One or two, sure, have lettuce and chard. One even has stepping stones and a wicker chair. But most of those gardens are struggling. Some of them are empty, with nothing but dirt and dandelions and thistles."

So Mom logged onto the library computer and she Twittered and Facebooked and Craigslisted for tools, plants and seeds. Because we had a "rolling address," she gave people the Sandwich Shack coordinates to mail stuff to. And if the stuff was too big or difficult to mail, she said to take them by the BMX park and leave them with The Kids. Clem and I were to be at the park from four to seven every day for a week.

Well, people reposted Mom's post, and word got around. By the end of the week, Mom had a rake and a shovel and a bunch of hand tools and plants and packages of seeds. While Clem and I biked the circuits, Mom worked in her "found" community-garden plot. Just one month later, we had parsley, lettuce and kale. We set up at a picnic table in one of the city parks and cooked the kale on our Coleman stove, with olive oil and sesame seeds sprinkled on top, and it was good. Really good.

One problem though, was Mom's hands. She couldn't get the gunk out from under her nails. You can't serve sandwiches with grimy hands and wrists scratched up from blackberry canes. So Clem and I did a special bottle run—a big one, three hours—then biked all the way to the depot with what Clem called our Blue Box booty. Two hundred cans and bottles in one afternoon! Twenty dollars. We bought Mom a sweet pair of gloves. Leather, and they would not let a thorn through, the salesman told us.

Clem had his biking. Something he was good at. And I'd sit on the fence and watch. But after seeing that first slam at the Spiral Café, I had something to do too.

I had somewhere to be. In my head. In my heart. In my fingertips, drumming out the beat. In my mouth, feeling out the shapes of syllables. In my ears, listening.

Two days after that hot chocolate at the Spiral for the first time without Dad, I sat on the BMX park fence with my binder on my lap and my hand ticking across the page, pen scratching, ink looping, the lines on the loose leaf like tightrope wire, my words its acrobats.

"What did you think? Angie? Yoo-hoo! Snap out of it."

I looked up. Clem was breathing hard. His ginger freckles glimmered on his flushed face, matching the ginger hairs that curled out from under his helmet. I didn't really want to snap out of it though. I liked where I was. I was swimming in warm water, netting fish, most of them alive and colorful, a few white as bone and eerie.

"Did you like my new trick?"

I bit my lip. "I didn't see it."

"Let me do it again."

Clem pedaled off down the path between the bushes. He wound his way out of sight, then soared up in front of me. The bushes shook in his wake. Their tiny green buds were like little lanterns. There were hundreds. The longer I looked, the more I saw. It was like Clem's freckles, or the stars when we parked on the edge of town where it's dark—more and more, and *more* of them the longer you stare. I looked down at my notebook. Each letter on the page was a bud on a tree, or a dark star in a white night...

"Angie!" Clem called.

"Yeah!" I yelled back, my voice a lie, a shallow puddle. I stirred it up. "That was great!"

Clem pedaled up the next rise. I pretended he wasn't shaking his head in exasperation. No, he was just getting his ginger curls out of his eyes.

Dad

My father has the widest shoulders I have ever seen. One of his friends calls him Popeye, because that's him—skinny legs, narrow hips, long back and then *wham*, those wide shoulders. I rode on those shoulders plenty of times. It was like sitting in an armchair. Dad would hoist me up with one hand.

He would forget I was up there too. That's how strong he is. Once, he walked under a rose arbor while I was on his shoulders. My face got cut up from the thorns. He knelt by me saying, "Sorry, sorry, sorry." And, "stupid Daddy, stupid daydreaming Daddy." He tore a sleeve off his T-shirt, ran it under a tap and wiped my face so carefully.

Dad got his big shoulders from lifting rock and brick. One of his last jobs in Victoria was laying a path at a friend's house. I visited him there on my way home from school. Dad wasn't in the front, so I followed the path around to the back. The bricks zigzagged, spraying outward and then retreating inward. The path swirled and scrolled in on itself. It swooped this way and that as the bricks wound and unwound, then suddenly crisscrossed and tightened into a Celtic knot. It was magical.

I stood at the very center of the knot. The sun shone on me, piercing the chill of the afternoon. Sometimes, I wish that I had never left that spot.

But I did. Dad was in the backyard, crouching, which isn't unusual for a bricklayer. His head was lowered, and he was shaking. I didn't understand at first. Not until I heard him breathe in, making a sound like a backward laugh. A sob.

"Dad?" I asked, stepping closer.

Dad wiped his eyes on his sleeve. "Hi, honey. Just allergies."

"Allergies?"

"Yeah."

His voice was hoarse, raspy. He cleared his throat. He looked at me and smiled, then shoved a brick into the sand. It was the path's last brick. The path was finished. Dad stood, put his hands on his hips and stretched.

"That's that," he said. "Want a ride home?"

He was all pale, powdered with brick dust. There were lines through the dust beneath his eyes—tear tracks. Dad loaded his tools into his wheelbarrow. "Hop in," he said. He wheeled me—a trowel sticking into my back—to the road where he'd parked his friend's truck. He'd recently sold our own truck to raise money for food.

As we drove, I played the same question over and over in my head. *Dad, why were you crying?*

At a red light, Dad looked over at me and answered it. "Honey," he said. "You know that your mom and I are going through a tough time. I'm not making enough money."

"I know. I *know*." I wanted him to stop talking. He and Mom had been fighting lately. They had never fought much before—in fact, it was normal to find them hugging in the kitchen or holding hands on the couch and talking. With all the fighting, Clem and I had started going to the BMX track more often or holing up in the closet in his bedroom and playing Skip-Bo. It was hard to tell red from purple in the dark.

"I'm going away, sweetheart," Dad said.

"No."

"Just for a while. A friend in Ontario has work for me."

"*No.*"

"Not for long, honey."

Tears stung my eyes. "Is that why you were crying?"

"I don't want to leave you, sweetheart."

"But you *are* leaving me."

"For work. Only for work."

After supper, Dad and Clem went for a walk. When they came back, Clem's eyes were red and he went straight to his room, slamming the door behind him. Mom did not move. She stayed in the armchair by the big window overlooking the harbor. As she looked out, rain began to splash against the window. The raindrops rolled down the window, leaving wobbling paths. Mom took a deep breath.

Dad busied himself in the kitchen, whistling loudly. Next morning, he was gone. I could tell as soon as I woke up. The apartment felt like it had too much air. Empty air. On the breakfast table, Dad had left two envelopes, one with Clem's name, the other with mine. Inside my envelope was a goodbye note and fifty dollars. Clem got fifty too, and a note, but he's never shown it to me. I haven't shown him mine either. I feel like I'd ruin its spell if I showed it to anyone else. Spell? The love. Four months later, I still can't read it without crying. But I do. When I get a moment alone in the car, which isn't often, I pull the letter out and read its misspelled words.

Angela My Angel,
Do not worry about me Kid-o. I love you in my heart every second of every minute. Be good to your Mum.
See you online, right?
Your the best daughter a father could wish for. I love you.
Your dad.

I read the letter over and over, looking for words that say he will be back. But no matter how many times I read it, I never find them.

Pity

My heart drops every time I think about tonight's slam. I can't concentrate in class. I keep running my words through my mind, repeating them over and over. Then, before I know it, Mom's driving Clem and me to the Spiral Café. Clem's not happy about it.

"Everyone's pretentious! Precious! Puffed up. Preening," he complains.

"No, they aren't." I laugh. "They're profound! Poetic. Perceptive. Powerful."

"They *piss* me off."

"Well, they ins*pire* me."

"You lose."

"Whatever."

"Clem, keep your sister company. Remember, she spent Saturday afternoon at a bike park in Langford for *your* sake."

"Yeah," I say. "In the *rain.* And you didn't even win."

I mean to tease Clem, but he looks wounded.

"I was tired," he begs.

"I'm sorry—"

"My legs were stiff."

We go silent. Mom looks ten years older than she did a minute ago. Her mouth is tight, and she clenches the steering wheel. Even her skin looks dull. It's the wear of worry—and guilt.

Because, of course, Clem *is* tired and stiff. What kind of champion sleeps with his knees bent and the soles of his feet pressed against the cold vinyl of a car door? Clem's height is the saddest thing about living in the Skylark. Sometimes, in the middle of the night, he'll get out of the car just to stretch. Mom wouldn't let him for the longest time, saying it would draw too much attention. But finally she relented after Clem practically cried, his legs hurt so much. His whole body was hurting, even his underarms, he said. Sometimes, as we're falling asleep, he rolls his window down and sticks his legs out and wiggles his pale toes in the inky night.

When we pull up to the Spiral Café, Mom reaches into her purse and hands us a five.

"See you in two hours," she says. She has a cleaning job to get to. I hate it when she cleans. I'm afraid she'll hurt herself again.

We've learned to open and close the car doors quickly, so people don't see all the stuff inside. "Going camping?" people have asked. Or, "Moving day?" I'm worried that if people figure it out, they'll call social services and Clem and I will be put in a foster home. Mom says this won't happen—"The police left us alone, remember?" But I've heard stories about kids being taken from their parents just because there isn't a table in the house and the kids eat sitting on the floor. Anyway, it's cozy in the Skylark. The heater works fine. Mostly, we shut the door fast because we don't want the cold getting in.

The sidewalk is dark and empty. But the café is bright, thrumming with the people inside talking and laughing. On any other night, it would be comforting, but tonight my heart drops. It drops and drops, like a penny falling from the top of the Empire State Building, burning against the air. Like a bird, wings tucked in, bombing the surface of the water for a fish. A fish that it will miss.

"I'm nervous," I tell Clem.

"What about?"

I haven't told him about my poem. I didn't tell Mom either. I don't want to be cheered on. I just want to do it.

"I'm nervous too," Clem says.

"What are *you* nervous about?"

A clump of girls with pink hair and lip rings push past, laughing over an umbrella that won't close.

"Not really my crowd," Clem says, offering a quick, apologetic quarter-smile that I've seen cross Dad's face lots of times. "I don't belong in artsy-fartsy places."

I check him over. He's wearing skater gear from head to toe.

"You should have won that bike race," I say. "You're a phenom on the track."

"Whatever." He shrugs, then mumbles, "I need a coach."

"When we get that swimming pool."

It's our joke. It's as close as we come to saying, *Where the hell are we? Why are we living in a* car*? Without Dad?* The unspoken theory is this, if we can afford to see our lives inside a joke, then we'll be okay. We'll have a future.

A big guy wearing a bandanna and eyeliner, his sideburns trimmed into spirals, is collecting the entry fee. His T-shirt has a picture of a banana inside a circle. *Bananarchy*, it says.

"Three dollars," the guy tells us.

My mouth goes dry. Clem shoots me a troubled look.

"Each of us?" I ask.

"Unless you're performing."

"I'm performing," I say.

"Then it's free."

Clem elbows me. He's smirking, but his eyes are wide. *How are you going to get out of this lie?*

I just smile back. The big guy gives me a clipboard. My hand trembles as I add my name to the list. I think of my dream—our family name climbing that list for public housing. But here, it's not Kilpatrick. It's just me, Angie.

"Great, we've got two dollars for a night of fun," Clem hisses as we find a table at the back. "And how are you going to get your name off that list?"

"I'm not. I'm performing."

"No way."

"Wait and watch," I say. "And clap when I'm done."

Clem rolls his eyes. "I don't believe you."

"I'll just have water," I say.

"We could share a tea," Clem says, scanning the menu. "Wait, here's something…I'll be right back."

Clem heads to the counter to order. His jeans are baggy, and his band T-shirt—something overblown from Walmart—hangs from his shoulders in a way that makes me hurt. It's as if it's hanging from a hanger. Clem has gotten bony. Maybe he's going through a growth spurt. Stretching out.

I rehearse my piece in my head for the hundred-thousandth time. Last week, only one performer read from the page. The rest had their stories in their brains—whole paragraphs, whole pages. A few times, people got stuck. They forgot their words. They'd look up at the ceiling, then at the audience, and smile sheepishly. After ten seconds or so, the people in the audience would start snapping their fingers. It was a way to offer support—they were holding the beat of the piece. It's neat to hear a dozen people snapping their fingers. It's warm and low, like rocks knocking under the waves at the beach. Or maybe it's the sound moths make to themselves when they bat their furry little wings. The finger snapping really seemed to help—the performers came around. They'd break into smiles and raise a finger—*Right, got it!*—and they'd dive back in. The snapping would fade away.

If I forget my words, I don't think I'll find my way again. It took me three days to write my poem or whatever it is. The next three days, I recited it over and over, fixing little mistakes here and there, cutting a word or choosing a better one. I was mostly laying the track though, burning it into my brain so it wouldn't fall apart while I slept. I wanted to get to a point where the words were all mine, forgettable as my own fingers, forgettable as my tongue, so I could then *perform* them—bend them, whisper or shout them without getting muddled.

I didn't imagine that I'd be feeling this fevered with nerves. I'll have to take my cheat sheet up to the stage with me after all. I wish Clem would hurry back. I need him to hide me a little. Twig Girl approaches the mic. The café goes quiet.

"Good evening," Twig says. "A full house. New names on the sign-up list too. We're trending, I guess. Going viral. Contagion of the spoken word. And there ain't no vaccination. No shot, no potion, no pill, no serum. No cure. You'll be stained, you'll be spoiled. You'll also be cleansed, mended, glorified, even blessed. Yes! You will be freed."

Twig smiles mischievously. She dips her head, and the crowd applauds. The first performer is an older guy in his twenties with a goatee. I don't hate a lot of things, but goatees look like pubic hair. Pubic hair on a person's face is not a good thing.

"Remember these?"

Clem's finally back. He's carrying two little cups of hot chocolate.

"Kid size. A dollar each. You don't have to be a kid to order them."

Clem doesn't seem embarrassed at all. But then he raises an eyebrow at me, quick and light, and his smile turns sad. I know what he's saying. He's asking me, *Is this going to end? How long can we live on kid-size hot chocolate?*

I force a smile. Force it into my eyes. *We'll be fine.*

Goatee Man's performance piece is more a story than a poem. It's about a rat that chews through the walls of the White House and becomes Barack Obama's pet. At night, when everyone in the White House is asleep, the rat climbs up to Obama's pillow and gives him pro-rat advice like "Make farmers plant more corn" and "Rats aren't to blame for the bubonic plague—change the history books" and "Make rat catchers pay higher taxes." It's pretty funny. Not laugh-out-loud funny, but people chuckle and Goatee Man gets a good round of applause.

The next reader is old, with a white beard and glasses. He hasn't memorized his piece and fidgets with his pages, losing his place a bunch of times. It's about how family is important and how you've got to hold them close. But he just blurts it out. Even though it's an important idea, the way he tells it is boring. It's like a lecture, a big message that everyone got ages ago. As the old guy reads, Clem slides down in his chair. That's my cue. I reach into my coat pocket and pull out the chocolate bar I bought this morning with some of the money Dad left. Snickers, Clem's favorite. Clem sits up.

He's truly hungry. He eats the thing in three bites, in under a minute, barely chewing. Then he turns the wrapper inside out and licks it clean. I bite my lip. I feel more sad than embarrassed. When Clem finishes his hot chocolate, he reaches in with his pinky and wipes every last bit from the sides of the cup. He sucks all the chocolate from his finger. When I finish my drink, he does the same with my cup.

After the old man, who gets light applause, is a guy about twenty. He has blond dreadlocks and is wearing shorts—in early April—and a hemp necklace strung with shells. His story is called "Tofino," and it's about getting hit on the head by his surfboard. In the story, he passes out, and while he's "under"—under the surface of the water, or unconscious—he has a love affair with a mermaid. They get married and everything. One night he wakes from a terrible weight on his chest. His mermaid wife is sitting on him, urgently trying to wake him because he has to go to the surface or he'll die.

The surfer is devastated to leave "that place of perfect happiness, a place where you never cry, because you are already living in a giant tear." Eventually, he breaks through the surface of the water, back into the air.

The pain in my lungs is horrible. I'm sobbing.

My surfing partner grabs me. "Man, was I worried," he says. "You were down there for, like, a whole minute."

I stare at him. I want to tell him what happened, where I've been. I touch my face, but there are no tears. Only ocean water.

People clap like crazy when the guy's finished.

Next up is the girl who wrote about "where mercy grows." Her new piece is about the loose shingles on her apartment building that flap in storms. In her poem, she's lying in her bed, waiting for the entire roof to fly off. She says, "Exposure's around the corner. It will fly in on the next ragged wind." She even sings at one point.

When she's finished, I look over at Clem to see if he realizes how good Mercy Girl's poem was. He's reaching for a plate of food from the next table.

"Are you sure they're not coming back?" I ask.

"Positive. They took their coats and left as soon as Poor Exposed Me started telling her story."

Clem plunks two plates onto our table—one has half a bagel and cream cheese, the other has three-quarters of a raspberry square. Clem digs in. He doesn't offer me any, but I don't mind. I'm too nervous to eat. Then I notice

Surfer Boy across the room, staring at me and Clem. Is he going to tell the café owners about Clem taking the food? Is it that big a deal? The food was just going to be thrown away.

Twig has refreshed her red lipstick. "Looks like we have a first-timer tonight," she says. My heart clunks to the bottom of my rib cage. I breathe deep, trying to pull it back up. "Please welcome Angie."

As I take ten wobbly steps to the mic, I pat my back pocket, making sure the script is there. The café is totally silent. I can hear my blood pumping. It's like listening to a conch shell. Twig adjusts the mic to the right height, then nods and smiles. Her smile puts air into my sails.

"I was thinking about the poem last week that, um, the last reader performed," I start. My voice sounds far away.

It's clear, water-clear, but trembling. "About that field 'where mercy grows.' I tried to figure out what mercy is, what it looks like and feels like. But all I came up with is what it isn't."

In my mind's eye, the words of my poem scroll past, black letters painted on a white wall. This was how I imagined them when I memorized them. I watch the words flow past, but I can't speak. I swallow. It's like I have to lower my tongue into my neck to find my voice, to get it to spark. I look at Clem. He nods. He smiles. And there's my voice, dragged up against the side of my throat.

I don't know what mercy is, but I have met pity. Pity is a wilted flower. A rusting blade. It would cut you if it wasn't so pathetic. Pity doesn't smell good. If mercy is oasis, pity is penitentiary. Pity is bitter, a bite of something rotten.

Even while pity's eyes well up, brim with do-goodness, pity sneers. Pity is so small it has no heart. Pity is all the rich have to offer—they hold it toward you, a dead, mangled bird in their hands, a little bundle of sorriness. Oh, how good pity feels, its sticky warmth, its sickly charm. But pity sits in the gut, souring, like guilt. Pity puts you in your place. It can't call you home. Poor, poor, poor, poor pity.

As I speak, my voice rises. It stretches thin and wavers. My face feels like it's being stung by wasps. I run out of breath. My words crack. My heart, well, it's a wrecking ball. It tries to break through my ribs, make a run for it. I stick it out though. I don't vomit and I don't forget a word. I don't pull out my cheat sheet. And when I'm done, the audience doesn't look at me with pity.

They clap! Somehow, my rubber legs carry me back to our table, where Clem sits, freaked out.

"Did I embarrass you?" I ask.

"No," Clem answers. "I'm just—when did you learn to do that?"

I shrug. "This week?"

"It was good, Angie," he says quietly. "You said things I felt when the cops used to bring us stuff, or when that old friend of Mom's pats us on the head but never invites us in. You made me feel all that again."

"Sorry."

"No. I thought I was the only one who felt that way."

Two others perform after me, but I can barely pay attention. My mind keeps racing back to those terrifying moments onstage. I remember every word I stumbled on and, better, the sweet feeling of the words I nailed. But I shake my head to clear it—I want to hear the others. I listen double, once for the story, once for how they built it.

Finally, Twig introduces the week's judges, the owners of the hair salon next door. While they deliberate, Clem stops the surfer as he passes our table and asks if his mermaid story was true. The surfer shrugs. "What is truth anyway, man?" he asks. Then he stares at me as if he's angry. It takes the wind out of my sails—punches a hole right through them, actually, and my confidence flies out through that hole.

"It was a cool story," Clem says.

The guy with the ragged sweater, Aaron, the reigning champion, taps my elbow.

His eyes are light blue, almost chalky.

"Hey," he says. "Cool."

"Thanks."

"*Moon! Moon! I am prone before you. Pity me, and drench me in loneliness*," the guy says. "That's the poet Amy Lowell."

"It's beautiful," I say. *Amy Lowell. I will google her at the library*. "You didn't perform tonight."

"I couldn't come up with anything. Fallow week." The guy points to his head. "Germinating. I've been reading. Priming the pump. You can't write if you don't read. Reading a lot is the difference between those who win and those who don't."

Mercy Girl passes by.

"Hey," I say. "Your thing was really good."

"My *thing*?"

"Your, uh, slam piece."

"Right. Yours too."

"The idea of the roof flying off. I like that."

"Yeah," Mercy Girl says. "You going to write about that too, next week? Or about a floor that's falling or something?"

"No. I don't think so." Then I get it. She doesn't like that I riffed off her poem. "I just thought your poem last week was so good. It inspired me. I was answering it."

"Echoing it."

"I wasn't copying it."

Clem looks back and forth from me to Mercy Girl, like he's watching a tennis game or the Skylark's windshield wipers.

"I'm sorry," I tell Mercy Girl. "I didn't mean to—"

"Hmm." Mercy Girls grunts and walks away.

Clem shakes his head. "*Boo hoo! You copied my moves!* I hear that all the time at the BMX park. Just ignore it. Where do they think they got *their* moves?"

"Keep your eye on the prize, hey," I say.

We burst out laughing. It's something Dad used to say to tease Mom if she walked in on him in the middle of getting dressed. It's kind of disgusting but mostly hilarious.

The café hushes. Twig steps up to the microphone.

"Another interesting night at the Spiral Café," Twig says. "Third place this week goes to Violet. Great singing!"

The audience claps as Mercy Girl collects her prize, which is an old-style, secondhand game of Scrabble.

"Second place goes to—a first-timer. A slam virgin! Angie, for her piece 'Mercy.' I mean, 'Pity.' Pity's so small it doesn't have a heart—I like that line."

I'm totally shocked. Clem has to shove me out of my seat. Twig hands me a book called *Keep That Candle Burning*

Bright & Other Poems by a woman named Bronwen Wallace, and a dozen eggs donated by someone in the audience. The brown eggs are so big, the carton has to be held shut with a rubber band.

"And our winner this evening, Jeremy Loren, for 'Mermaid.' A great story, Jeremy. The ocean is a giant tear. Love it."

Surfer wins a paint-by-number picture of a matador, on velvet, and a haircut at the salon next door. The audience laughs at this, since it doesn't look like Surfer's going to part with his dreadlocks anytime soon. But Surfer doesn't laugh. He actually looks put out. As he walks back to his table, he pushes past me, nearly knocking my eggs out of my hand. I look up, thinking he'll apologize, but he just sneers. When I look for Mercy Girl to congratulate her, she's already heading out the door.

I don't think I should have gotten second place. Mercy Girl's piece was better than mine. Maybe the judges felt sorry for me. Maybe they gave me their pity vote.

Home

"Let's boil those eggs when we get home," Clem says.

"Home?" I ask.

"You know what I mean."

Clem suddenly stops. We're in front of an apartment window at sidewalk level. It's a blazing rectangle of yellow in the dark night. "Look."

Inside the apartment, a large man in sweatpants reclines in an easy chair in front of a TV. A large yellow dog sleeps at his feet. Near them is a bookcase filled with books, and two paintings hang on the wall, one of a river banked by forest, the other of a snow-filled meadow. It strikes me that the last thing I would want in our car would be pictures of cold, damp forest or snow. I'd want a picture of—well, of someone in an easy chair, watching TV. Of the inside.

"I don't miss TV," Clem says. "I don't mind watching a show now and then at Aunt Evie's, but it feels weird now, like I'm sticking my head in a box. I hate living in a car. I hate it. But when we get back to living inside, I'm going to *do* stuff. I'm going to start a business designing gear especially for cyclists, like a helmet that whistles when you hit a certain speed, or a handlebar attachment that records your laps."

"I'm going to write all over my bedroom walls," I say.

"Cool."

Mom, Clem and I have four favorite parking places. We spend two nights at each before moving on. Tonight, it's Blackberry Estates, a quiet lane beside a park where Clem and I, with Mom—and Dad—have picked blackberries since we were little. There's no public washroom nearby, which is a drag, but it's the quietest of the places we stay.

We've learned to make a little noise as we approach the car, so the person "at home" has some warning. In the early days, we gave each other a few heart attacks by appearing suddenly at the car window. When you're living in a car, some part of your brain is always on high alert. You can get cozy in the

Skylark, but don't mistake that coziness for privacy. You're never out of view. Sorry, Mercy Girl, but the shingles flew off my house long ago.

Mom's surprised but proud that I competed in the slam. She likes the eggs too. We set up the Coleman stove beside the car and boil up eight—three each for me and Clem, two for Mom. We eat them with crackers that Mom got at the Single Parent Resource Center and cups of mint tea that we make with the same water we boiled the eggs in. A few bits of egg white float to the top of my cup. I would never have put up with that in the old days, but we're experts now at conserving water.

Mom's spirits pick up as we eat. "What's that book you won?" she asks.

I click my flashlight and start to read from *Keep That Candle Burning Bright*. The book says they're poems, but they feel like letters. The writer just starts speaking right into your ear, telling you exactly what's on her mind. I can tell that Mom and Clem start thinking about other stuff, but it doesn't really matter whether they're listening. I just reel the words out into the night, lay them down like a carpet for us, let them build against the air like wallpaper.

Getting Clean

Our favorite library branches are the Bruce Hutchison and the Juan de Fuca. They're both next to swimming pools. It takes a little more gas to get to them since they're farther away, but Mom says it's worth the drive. We swim first, flying down the slides and leaping off the towers, but mostly we spend our time in the change rooms. In the hot showers, actually. Ahh! I shave my legs and scrub every square centimeter of my body. I leave the conditioner in my hair for minutes, not just one. I soap between my toes and twist the corner of my washcloth to deep-clean my ears, and I come out of there glowing. Clem too. We're so clean, it's like we've got fresh batteries. Mom walks out looking like *two* million bucks.

With our hair still wet and our eyes buggy from the chlorine, we head to the library. If we're at Bruce Hutchison, we don't even have to leave the building. At Juan de Fuca, we have to run thirty steps through the evening air and then we're inside again. I love approaching the yellow light of the library. It's like entering a warm cave. It's so kind in there. There's nothing you have to do or prove or pay for.

Mom tries not to hurry to the computer, but she's eager to check Gmail. She hears from Dad a few times a week. She is in a whole other world, a happier one, when she reads his letters. It's like she forgets where she is. That evening, as we're settling in to sleep, she'll announce, "Dad says his new apartment is over an ice-cream shop. The freezers hum all night," or, "He's putting a check in the mail for clothes for you two."

Dad and Mom always seemed to start in the middle of a conversation. Mom could say out of the blue, "No, I don't think we should do it," and Dad would answer, "Remember that guy in Austin? He'd say that we should go for it," and she'd say, "Yeah, but look how long that guy's beard was." And then the two of them would burst out laughing. From start to finish, Clem and I would have no idea what they were talking about. They had their storehouse of experiences and could talk in short-hand. Sure, sometimes they argued,

mostly over how they parented us—
Mom thought Dad was too soft, and
Dad thought Mom worried too much.

But during the last few months
in the apartment, they'd fought all
the time. Mom couldn't say anything
without Dad getting mad. Mom would
say, "My back hurts from cleaning,"
and Dad would answer sarcastically,
"Yeah, too bad your husband can't
bring home the bacon."

"That's not what I meant," Mom
would say.

"No?"

"No," Mom would say firmly.
"Liam. I love you."

At first, that would be enough. Dad
would say, "Yeah. Sorry. I just wish I
could find some work." Then they'd hug.

Dad would be patient for a while, but
then he would start reacting again. He'd
say things like, "I guess I'm not good
enough for you." Or, "You must regret

marrying a loser like me." Once, he called himself a "depressed laid-off bricklayer," which was a little over the top.

Mom finally lost her patience. "Look," she said once. "Maybe you need to try a different line of work."

Dad didn't like that. "I knew you never believed in me," he barked.

Mom sighed. "Stop making it about yourself. It's not your fault there aren't any jobs right now."

"I know where there's work."

"You do?"

"Yes," Dad said. He gave Mom a hard look. "Yes, Rebecca. I do."

They were the same words he'd said when they got married. But this time when he said them, Mom burst into tears.

We wash at Auntie Evie's on Wednesdays after school. Auntie Evie isn't really our aunt. Mom has no siblings, and Dad has two brothers who fish up in Alaska, but that's it for family. Aunt Evie is one of Mom's oldest friends. We lived with her and her husband, Mitch, for a week after we lost the apartment, but Evie finally had to tell us that it wasn't working out. She sat us down in the living room one afternoon and poured us glasses of pineapple juice. Why do I remember that so well? "I don't know how to tell you this…" she began. "I could have you live here for a long time, but Mitch is different. He needs his quiet. It's why we never had kids."

After she told us, we just sat there, drinking our juice in the quiet living room, getting a grip on the terror that *we had nowhere to go*.

We sneak into Auntie Evie's place. She washes our clothes in her building's laundry room and makes an early supper for us. It's nearly always spaghetti, but that's fine. We have to clear out before

Mitch comes home from work, but usually our laundry isn't dry yet. Auntie Evie folds it all, puts it in a garbage bag and leaves it around the back door. We're always nervous that we're going to run into Mitch when we go back to get it. We aren't nervous that Mitch will be mad that we're at the apartment. We just don't want him to feel guilty about needing his quiet. We know he likes us because he got his friend, who lives near the BMX track, to let us store our bikes in his garage. Uncle Mitch also found us the Skylark.

skylark

For Sale, 1982 Buick Skylark. Immaculate 2.8L V6—2nd Owner, Garage Kept—Clean Interior—Low miles—Original Owners' Manual and Floor Mats—Full Spare Tire, and a Few Extras!—Full Service and Maintenance Records for Over 10 Years. $2500.

Uncle Mitch paid for the Skylark. A couple grand is nothing to sneeze at, Mom said. She was able to accept Mitch's paying for the car, since Dad had helped Mitch and Evie lots of times. He even helped Mitch get his job.

Mitch got the Skylark for five hundred dollars below the asking price. Mom never asked why, but we guessed Mitch pulled a few sympathy strings— spotlight on a woman and two kids huddled on a piece of wet cardboard in a dark alley.

So we were a charity case. Charity is the other side of the pity coin, and we did not like the car at first for that reason. It's a thirty-year-old car, but in brand-new shape. We are careful with the uphol-stery. We respect the time the owner spent rubbing cream into its leather, vacuuming the car's carpets, oiling its door hinges.

The trunk is its most amazing feature—16.4 cubic feet. A "four-body trunk," Mitch called it. Our keepsakes are in there in boxes—pictures Clem and I drew in kindergarten, grade-school report cards, Dad's wedding cummerbund. When we left the apartment, we sold most of our stuff on Craigslist, including Mom's wedding dress. She still hasn't sold her wedding ring though—I check her finger nearly every day. The ring is twenty-two-karat gold, and the band is wide. "That is no regular bricklayer's wife's wedding ring," Dad used to joke.

Mom, Clem and I took the bus to pick up the Skylark. It was the middle of March. The seller lived in a boring neighborhood of small square houses and lawns cut as short as living room carpets. "Call me Graham," the old man said, leading us through his tidy house to the garage. Mom liked the car immediately. Clem and I saw its potential. "Let's put our allowances together and buy some twenty-two-inch rims for this baby," Clem deadpanned once Graham was out of earshot. Of course, the car won't ever be pimped, but making jokes about getting sheepskin for the seats, plush dice to dangle from the rearview, a performance muffler and colored headlights has become a game for us.

The car was ours whether we liked it or not. The money had been paid. The deal was done. Mitch and Auntie Evie were going to pay the insurance for four months, and then Mom would be on the hook for it. Graham could have handed us the keys and waved goodbye from inside his garage, but instead he invited us in for tea and biscuits. He had already prepared a tray with cups and the full teapot. We perched on the couch in his neat living room as a clock on the mantel ticked unevenly—tick-TOCK, tick-TOCK, tick-TOCK.

"May I?" Clem gestured toward the piano.

"Be my guest."

Clem played Pachelbel's *Canon in D Major,* but something kept going wrong. Clem repeated a phrase, then poked a single key over and over.

"Broken hammer," Graham said between sips of tea.

"I'll dance around it," Clem said.

"My wife, Florence, was the pianist," Graham said. "Don't suppose you're in the market for a piano too? Going cheap."

"No," Mom said. "We don't need a piano."

"Right," Graham said, clearly remembering why we needed the car. "I don't suppose you do. Sorry."

"That's all right," Mom said. "We can't thank you enough. It's a really nice car."

"I'd polish it up on Sunday mornings, and then Florence and I would go for a long drive," Graham said. "Set ourselves free."

"Sure," Mom said.

Clem cleared the plate of cookies.

Then Graham jangled the keys toward us.

"Here you go," he said. "You drive carefully."

Now, when Clem and I are too rambunctious in the car, wrestling or being too loose with our mugs of hot chocolate that Mom makes in the kettle that plugs into the cigarette-lighter socket, Mom says, "Hey, hey, remember Florence." It works. I think of Florence, who must have been proud of her car. I think of Graham too, vacuuming the seats every Sunday. I imagine the two of them watching us, and I quiet down.

I pay Clem five dollars to go to the slam with me. He grumbles, but not as much as I thought he would. When Mom drops us off, I notice Surfer, surrounded by girls and acting cool.

With the extra money, Clem buys soup, a toasted bagel and two kid-size hot chocolates. I hear him ask for extra butter for his bagel, and I hurt inside. Clem needs all the fat he can get.

I say hi to Mercy Girl, and she nods. That's something, at least. The first reader's piece is about washing a cat in the kitchen sink. She uses the verb *claw* a thousand times. She could have used so many others—clutch, scratch, grip, seize, snag, snare. Reading Bronwen Wallace and Amy Lowell in the library, I have learned that every word counts. You have to *wring* your poem after you first get it on the page, squish the extra water out of it— the repetitions and boring words—boil it down, reduce it to its flavorful parts.

Listen to the sounds too. Forget what the words mean and just listen for rhymes. A rhyme doesn't have to be at the end of a line. It can be anywhere—it's just a sound repeating. *Dark* and *lark* can rhyme, but so can *darn* and *lark* or *darn* and *dark* or *lark* and *lurk*. Words can rhyme in the middle, or at the start. Alliteration—the two *w*'s in Walt Whitman—is a kind of rhyme. *Walt* and *Whit* also rhyme—both short syllables starting with *w* and ending in *t*. Rhyme is everywhere, rhyme is fine, rhyme buffs and shines, it unites and entwines.

Surfer's story is really good this week, but every time he hits a cool line, he shoots me a look, as if he's saying, *So there*. His story is about how he and a friend survived an avalanche when they were skiing, how they swam with the snow and came out of the long rush of white perfectly naked.

The avalanche had "skinned" the clothes off him. "Thought I was going to die, but instead, I was reborn," he finishes, to huge applause.

Mercy Girl is up next. My heart starts pounding as she recites her piece. It's about a new car. What a crazy coincidence. It's about driving away from the car lot, feeling like "the road has just started" and "you've got a whole new body." Then she says, "but as you travel forward, feeling you could go anywhere, the weight of the car, of engine and glass and oil, starts holding you a little too well, pinning you down." Her piece ends,

> I stepped into that car lot,
> money thick in my pockets.
> I handed it over only to learn
> you can't ever go fast enough,
> there's a limit to living—
> always some kind of finish line.

Ever since I've started writing slam poems, English class makes sense to me. Mercy Girl was using the car as a metaphor for life. And that finish line? Well, everyone knows what that is.

People like Mercy Girl's poem. They clap and cheer. Meanwhile, Clem shifts in his seat, attentive to the people at the next table, who are reaching for their jackets. As soon as they leave their table, Clem swoops in on their unfinished desserts. Surfer approaches a moment later.

"Trying to get Hep B?" he asks Clem.

"I won't," Clem snarls between chews.

"That was rude, Clem," I say once Surfer's gone.

"It isn't his business what I eat," Clem said. "That guy is stuck up. Yeah, his head's stuck up his butt. Full of himself, get it?"

It's not like Clem. He doesn't go for the crude.

"Are you all right?" I ask.

"Did you get a note from Dad?" Clem answers.

I suck in my breath. I don't want to think about today's Facebook message.

"Yeah," I say. "I got it."

Dad's words swarm my head, but I've got to press them back. There's only room right now for my slam piece.

"A nice apartment, new friends…" Clem says.

"Yeah, I heard," I say.

"Sounds like he's got a new home."

"*Clem*," I say. I want him to stop. I've got to focus.

Aaron is next up on the stage. He delivers a rant about sharp things— knives and saws and broken glass. The rant slows down and ends as a reluctant love song to knowing the difference between good and bad, "divisions that create things whole, the scalpel cutting away what's diseased, or cutting the cord, making me, making you."

Suddenly, it's my turn. I'm more nervous than last week. One reason is that Surfer's looking at me sourly and Mercy Girl's staring me down. I'm nervous that my piece will upset her. What were the chances that our poems would both be about new cars? I look to Clem for encouragement. He's in another world. I widen my eyes to say, *Come on!* He gives me a lame thumbs-up. It's something, at least, and I start.

"Broken Hammer."

"Louder!" someone yells.

Twig adjusts the mic. "Just nerves," she whispers. "Imagine that you're telling it to just one person. Talking to a friend."

Dad floats into my mind. That's it.
I'll just talk to Dad, as if I'm writing
him a Facebook message.

"Broken Hammer," I repeat, clear
and sure.

After Mom and the old man
shake hands in the tidy garage
the old man offers me
the last apple on the apple tree.
"Careful now," he says,
"last time I bit into an apple
I left a tooth inside."
I pick the heart-shaped apple
and as I do my toe nudges
another in the grass.
It's Saturday afternoon
we're checking out a ride
a 1982 Buick Skylark
only it's heavy, grounded, not at all
like a skylark, that bird of lightness
of flying high and diving low.

It was Florence's ride, Florence
the man's late wife.
Late? She won't be showing up.
In the living room as Mom signs the
    deed
a clock ticks on the mantelpiece
its mechanical heart off-balance—
tick-TOCK tick-TOCK tick-TOCK
as if the man's house is on a slant
    now
the pendulum called somewhere
    deeper.
"Do you want to buy the piano,
    too?" he jokes.
"Florence played. Saturday
    afternoons—"
the old man forces a smile
    and I get a shock, a little intake
    of breath
seeing the gap in his teeth, the hole
    in his heart where the wind blows
    through.

I approach the piano and play the
*   only song I know—*
a simple song, learned in school.
I glance at the old man—
he's smiling, practically airborne.
But one ivory key doesn't work.
The hammer is broken.
My finger pushes and pushes
but every time the song lands there
it dives down, down into silence
silence hidden in the grass
a silence where birds go
and apples lie on their sides.

The café stays quiet after I finish. I bite my lip—have I messed up? No. People are nodding thoughtfully. Then they clap for a long time. On the way back to my table, Mercy Girl catches my eye. She looks angry. Surfer is sitting with her, and he looks angry too. I don't get it. But others smile.

Their eyes follow me. Like I'm famous or something. Like they admire me. I'm relieved when the next person takes the stage. I like my privacy.

"That was weird," Clem whispers. "Good weird."

"How?"

"Lots of that story was true—lots of it really happened. But I played the piano, not you, and the guy, Graham, wasn't missing a tooth. And there was no apple. Where did you get all that?"

"I don't know," I say. "I just flip my memories over, bend and twist and mash them together. It's like dreaming, but I'm awake."

"Whatever," Clem says, smiling.

But he's not making fun of me. He's telling me it's cool. He seems to know what I'm on about.

"You do the same on the track," I say. "You bend and flip and twist."

"That's right," Clem says. "We're in the air, both of us, making up dreams."

At the end of the night, I try to talk with Mercy Girl in the washroom lineup. "Pretty funny both our slam poems were about buying cars, hey?"

"Yeah, right," Mercy Girl answers. "That line about wind blowing through the hole in the guy's heart. 'Everyone can see the wind blow…' That's straight from Paul Simon's song 'Graceland.' Didn't you think people would notice?"

"I was, like, sampling," I say.

Mercy Girl's shoulders relax. "Oh."

"But maybe it wasn't such a good choice. Maybe not everyone knows it."

"I know it. My mom has that CD," Mercy Girl says.

"My mom has it too," I say.

Mercy Girl smiles. She actually smiles! I smile back, but then a wave of hopelessness ripples through me. I get a picture of Mercy's mother dancing to Paul Simon in a sun-filled living room. Then I imagine *my* mother, squished in the front seat, listening to "Graceland" through the cheap, tinny speaker of our old iPod. I can't make friends with Mercy Girl. Because one day, she'll want to come to my house. We don't have room for visitors.

Payday

Every second Saturday is payday. We start the day by cleaning "the house." We repack our stuff, bundle up garbage, wash down the dash and console. We drive to the gas station and buy two gold-colored tokens that we plug into a big outdoor vacuum cleaner beside the gas pumps. I hate hearing the *clink-clank* of things going up the hose.

What did I just rob ourselves of? An earring? A quarter? I have to decide it was nothing more than a bobby pin or a penny. Why bother worrying that I've lost something valuable when I have no idea whether I did?

My mind has always wandered, but since I started doing slams, I pay attention to where it goes. And where it goes seems to be where the stories and poems are. Musing. Daydreaming. Remembering. Inventing. Figuring. Fancying. What-iffing. Picturing. Reliving. Unpacking. Searching. Idling. Considering. Contemplating. Speculating. Tripping. I write it all down in my binder with the stars and Sharpie hearts and the little brown bird with the crest on its head. I started on the last page of the binder and have been working back toward the middle. Soon my pages of what-iffing will meet my notes from math. And then what? My binder will explode.

An explosion doesn't seem all that impossible, actually. Ever since I started going to slams, I've been reading poems and essays (my English marks have improved), and it's been like explosion after explosion in my head. Walls tumbling down. I can go anywhere. It's like Clem rolling down the car window and sticking his legs out for a stretch. I can sit in the backseat of our dark cave of a car, hunched and barely moving, but I'm a million miles away. I'm freed from our little car, our compressed lives, our waiting for that municipal housing address.

On payday, after we have vacuumed the Skylark, Mom fills the tank—*full*—and we drive. Sometimes we motor all the way over the Malahat, stopping at the top to look down onto the inlet, the birds swooping *beneath* us. Sometimes we carry on to Bright Angel Park, where we cross the suspension bridge,

Clem stomping his feet and making the bridge swing and bolt, Mom and me running and screaming. Usually, Clem and I strip down and wade into the river. Even in late winter, we'll do it. The water is so clean and clear, we can see each other's entire bodies under the surface, every toe. We have a rule that we have to get our hair wet, have to dunk our heads, which ring afterward. It's like we've rebooted our brains. Payday offers a fresh start.

On the way back into town, we stop for supper. We *never* do drive-through. We take any chance to get *out* of the car. We'll go into A&W or Denny's. Last payday, we went to the Old Spaghetti Factory with a two-for-one coupon. Mom has gotten really good at clipping coupons. Clem and I ate every last bite of the minestrone soup, spaghetti and spumoni ice cream. Mom had a Caesar salad.

"Too bad Dad isn't here," I said. It just came out. Dad always used to be with us when we went to the Old Spaghetti Factory, which was usually for someone's birthday. He'd moon over the old farm tools on the walls and explain to us what they were used for. "We had one of those. I remember my poor dad working with it, colorful words flying out of his mouth. That part always came loose, see?" Mom would have a Caesar salad then too. Through-line.

"I wish he was here too," Mom said quietly. "He misses you two, you know that."

"Yeah, I know that," I said. "He misses you too. He says so every letter."

"Does he?"

I gulped. "He tells me to look after you," I said.

"He tells me the same thing," Clem said.

Mom smiled. "And he tells me to look after you two."

After supper at the Old Spaghetti Factory, we drove along the ocean to the terminal where the cruise ships dock on their way between California and Alaska. We parked as close as we could to MS *Amsterdam*. The giant cruise ship towered over us. Mom pointed out the disks on the giant ropes tying it to shore.

"They stop the rats from getting on board and traveling port to port," Mom said. "If they'd had those a few hundred years ago, there wouldn't have been the bubonic plague."

A station wagon was parked next to us. A couple sat in the front seats, and there was a kid in the back, about twelve years old. They were eating supper— it looked like burritos—from takeout wrappings. The car was packed with stuff—clothes and books and dishes.

I was up front with Mom. I angled the rearview so Clem could see me. We often adjust the mirror so we can see each other as we talk. In the early days, we'd crane our necks and look back, but we've evolved. I gestured toward the car next door. Mom was going on about how ship design changed after the plague while Clem and I just stared. Another family living in a car. They could have just been traveling on a road trip, but I didn't think so. They looked too much like they had nowhere to go. How many of us are there?

We gawked for a while longer at the cruise ship looming over our heads and at the passengers coming and going, all of them looking overfed and slow.

"These folks pay a thousand dollars for the joy of being cooped up," Mom said. "I've heard that after the first two days of all-you-can-eat and swimming in the pool, they get bored and start to drink."

"They should have a BMX track on the top. That would be wicked," Clem said.

"I thought we'd sleep at Marifield tonight," Mom said, turning the key in the ignition. The red dashboard lights went on and the engine revved high. "It's like starting up a submarine," Graham had said when he first showed us the car. "The red glow, the dials and gauges, engine revving like it's going into the unknown."

Marifield is just a block long, with small houses and an apartment block. One of the houses seemed to be abandoned. We parked beside it and peed in the backyard bushes. We like Marifield because it's close to school. Mom often drives us to school while we're getting dressed and eating breakfast—that's one of the perks of living in a car. Of course, she drops us off a few blocks from school—I would die if anyone at school saw me being dropped off.

On our way to Marifield, we passed the parking lot where carriage horses are led after a day pulling tourists through the city. They're fed there and watered as they wait, restless, tails flicking, to be loaded onto a trailer that will take them out of the city for the night, to the farm where they belong, where they can sleep. I watched them standing in the moonlight, free of the carriage and their cumbersome bridles. They stamped their feet every so often, shook their manes. I felt sad as I watched them. I felt wistful. They were like me and Mom and Clem—they had each other, but they weren't quite home.

Scars

I've gone to eight slams so far and placed second or third in three of them. I'm careful each week to come up with something new, something no one else has done. Mercy Girl made me anxious about imitating others, but that might be a lucky thing. It means I've got to figure out exactly what the other performers are doing so I don't just do the same. I especially don't want to imitate the hollow, empty delivery a lot of the slammers use, ending their lines with a rise in pitch as if they're asking a question. Clem can't stand it. Somehow, he figured out the problem. "They're just saying the words," he said. "They aren't thinking about what the words mean. Here's some advice. Every word you say, make it real. Like, if you're saying fridge, picture a fridge."

So I do. I even imagine my hand on the sticky handle of that fridge. I invest energy in every word. If a word can't take any energy, then maybe I need to cut it.

I'm also careful not to use words that keep coming up in other people's slam pieces. *Shards* is a favorite of theirs, and *scars*.

I think about scars all the time. Scars are zippers—you open them up and a story tumbles out. When Mom is done putting on her makeup and brushing her hair in the morning, she turns the mirror so I can use it from the backseat. Sometimes, the morning light bounces off and brings to my eyes the shining dots on my forehead where the rose thorns went especially deep that day I went through the arbor and Dad kneeled before me.

The scars remind me of the day Mom fell off the ladder. Mom was on the couch with her hand on her forehead, and Dad kneeled on the floor beside her. She told Dad she'd fallen while washing windows at the big house in Fairfield and how, luckily, the woman she was working for drove her home.

"Didn't she take you to a hospital?" Dad asked.

"She said I didn't need a hospital. Said I was fine. And I am. I will be."

Mom tried to sit but couldn't.

"I'll make supper," Dad said.

We had grilled-cheese sandwiches and cucumber slices for supper, all of us in the living room, since Mom wasn't about to move to the table. Dad had to fish around in the junk drawer for a bendy straw so she wouldn't have to lift her head too much. Clem and I sat on the floor, and Dad pulled the armchair up close to Mom. Dad was still in his work clothes, the dust all over him glowing white as the sun went down and the living room darkened. Mom never moved off the couch that evening. Dad got her painkillers from the drugstore and fed her a couple every few hours. Mom fell asleep, and we tiptoed around.

In the morning, Clem and I got our own breakfasts and made our lunches for school. After that, Mom didn't work for over two months.

When I think about it, that was the evening everything changed. That's when the swerving and the veering started, the fighting between Mom and Dad, then Dad selling his truck, the truck he was so proud of.

That last night Dad was home, when he said "I do" and Mom burst into tears, Dad said, "That woman should have taken you to the hospital. We should have sued her for having you work on an old ladder that was about to break."

"She didn't know it was going to break," Mom said between her tears.

"It wasn't right," Dad argued.

"*You* could have taken me to the hospital," Mom said. "*You* could have gotten angry with her. I was down for the count." Her voice was quieter as she added, "And I didn't want to cause trouble."

"Me neither," Dad confessed. "Neither of us is really the fighting kind. We're too gentle, Rebecca. One of us has to start making some trouble."

Mom laughed at that.

"I mean it, Rebecca," Dad said. But he put on a funny face and repeated, all Humphrey Bogart, "One of us has to start making some trouble."

The two of them laughed. Mom reached out and squeezed Dad's hand. As she did, my heart hurt like it had never hurt before, like it was being clenched by the whole cold universe. Both my parents had tears in their eyes.

A few weeks ago, as Mom laid the cutting board across the console for the night to join the front seats into a kind of bed, her necklace got caught in her hair.

"Sweetheart," she said. It was all she had to say. When you live in a car, three of you in a space the size of a closet, you don't have to say much to get each other's attention. I leaned over and untangled the necklace as gently as I could. Mom was wearing a new blouse, something from the Single Parent Resource Center clothing exchange, something too big, too loose. I could see down her collar. That was the first time I saw the scars on her back—two thick, red scars. I'm sure they're from her fall that day when the ladder rung broke. What I imagine is that the broken ends of the rung dragged against her as she went down.

I keep thinking I'll ask Mom about the scars, but I don't. The scars are Mom's secret. There are other secrets she doesn't tell. I know this because she is often quiet and because she greets us with a smile every morning and every afternoon after school and when she reaches over the driver's seat to lay her hand on our foreheads and say goodnight. She never talks about painful things, like about her father dying when she was ten. Or about not finishing school. Or about making so many mistakes on the till at Sandwich Shack that they replaced the words on the buttons—*tomatoes, olives*—with little pictures of the different vegetables. Or about her husband leaving her to find rough work in an unknown place. Or about sleeping in the front seat of an old car each night, her hip supported by a thrift-store cutting board.

Semifinals

Clem has had it. He won't come to the slam tonight, and Mom says she can't make him.

"He's gone with you lots of times, Angie. He's done his duty."

"He likes it," I say.

"No, I don't."

"You like the free food."

"Shut up."

"*Clem,*" Mom scolds. "What free food?"

"The food he—"

"Shut up!" Clem repeats.

"What food?" Mom asks again.

Clem gives me a sharp look. "Just because you want me there," he hisses. "It isn't all about you."

I relent. "They put out snacks once in a while."

"Oh," Mom says. "Well, Clem needs an evening to rest. He has time trials coming up."

"I know," I say. "But I've got semifinals this week."

"You'll do fine," Mom says. "I know you will."

So Clem gets dropped off at the park to practice, and Mom leaves me outside the Spiral with two dollars and fifty cents. Surfer and Mercy Girl are sitting at a table near the front, but they don't invite me to sit with them. In fact,

I'd swear that Surfer sticks his foot out for a split second as if to trip me. Every table is taken, so I stand at the back. I try to go through my poem in my head, but I can't concentrate. I feel nervous and exposed without Clem.

Mercy Girl gets called up to the stage. She approaches the mic with a sheet of paper in her hands. Her poem is about a girl who thinks her boyfriend has cheated on her. After a few lines, Mercy Girl tears the paper in half. "Why would you trample my innocence like that, why would you be so guilty?" To find out if her boyfriend is sneaking around, the girl reads her boyfriend's diary.

Mercy Girl continues to tear the paper in half and half again as she continues the story. After reading her boyfriend's diary, the girl says she feels "torn" for having been so sneaky and untrusting. She's also "torn up" by the words on the page, which—this is a funny bit—"are not all about another girl who's more fun than me. They're not about how quiet I get sometimes, or how worried, or that pimple I had last week. What you write in your diary, oh sweetheart, is the score of every game your basketball team played this season. That is all."

Mercy Girl tears up the last bits of paper. "*I'm* the guilty one. I have torn us apart. Now we are nothing but pieces. Pieces of the past."

Aaron is up next. His piece asks, what if there was Facebook during the French Revolution? It's funny. "*Like* if you think we should storm the Bastille. *Comment* if you think we should continue with the beheadings."

Surfer tells a magical story about a whale who cannot sing. Then it's my turn. My piece is about Skylark's glove compartment, about how small it is but how I like to imagine it's a portal to somewhere enormous. "Every time I pinch the latch, I think this time, it will let me in, let me through, to a ballroom, or outer space, glittering and expanding."

But I stumble over my words. I forget my lines. People snap their fingers, but I eventually have to reach into my pocket and, for the first time, read my piece. The paper shakes in my trembling hands. The tears in my eyes don't help either.

"Hey," Mercy Girl says when I'm finally off the stage. "Everyone has a tough night. Why don't you sit with us?"

"Thanks," I say.

Surfer doesn't move his backpack from the other chair. I slide a chair over from the next table. Surfer stares at me, smiling tightly. Gloating.

"That was terrible," I say.

"You just—lost your confidence," Mercy Girl says. "Don't be so hard on yourself. This game has its highs and lows. And a bit of fear isn't a bad thing.

Better than always thinking you're God's gift, you know?" Mercy Girl shoots a glance at Surfer and winks at me.

"Yeah," I say. "I think I do."

We smile at each other like old friends. Surfer misses it completely. He just sits there with his nose in the air.

"Your piece was good tonight," I tell him.

"Uh. Yeah."

He doesn't look at me. He never does, except when he nails a good line onstage. I realize that except for the first night, I've placed ahead of him every time. Is that why he's so put out?

"What did you think of Angie's piece?" Mercy Girl asks Surfer.

"Interesting," he answers. "Another poem about a car. That's three now."

"So?" Mercy Girl asks.

"So I know something about Angie that she probably wouldn't like people to know."

My body stiffens. I try to smile. "Oh, yeah?" I say, trying to sound light and breezy.

"I saw you last night, Angie. On Marifield Avenue. I saw your—your house."

"You did?" I can hardly talk.

Surfer's voice turns bitter. "Your house is close to the road, isn't it? Like, super close, squished right up to the curb?"

If Clem was here, he would rescue me. He'd get Surfer talking about something else, like surfing at Jordan River. Luckily, Twig is at the mic to announce tonight's winners. Even though I froze onstage, I come in third. Aaron comes in second— it's the first time he's ever competed and not won first place. Mercy Girl wins. Her prize is a fondue set. Aaron wins a pair of fuzzy dice—lucky him—and I win a deck of cards and a cribbage board, which are actually things we could use. Our deck is missing two cards, and we keep score with paper and pen.

Twig reminds us that summer is around the corner and Slam Night will soon be winding down for the year. She's tallied our standings for the season. Aaron, Mercy Girl, Surfer and I and three others are to compete next week in the year's finals.

I'll have to work hard, but Clem needs help with a time-trials event on the weekend. He has borrowed a camera from the school's camera club and wants me to shoot him and also be a one-person pit crew, ready to change a tire if needed. And he wants me to bike the course and give him my take—where to take things easy, where to go for broke.

"Everyone's asking for you at the bike park," he told me. "They're calling me The Kid now. There's no more The Kids. When was the last time you got on your bike?"

I can't remember.

It's a warm spring evening, still light. I don't need my flashlight to reach the car, which is parked in our new favorite place, a quiet road close to a bicycle trail. Mom is in the front seat, knitting, and Clem's in the back, bent over a textbook. I whistle as I approach the car to warn them.

Mom and Clem look up, smiling. Smiling big. They've been waiting for me. They have news.

"Our name reached the top of the list," Mom says.

I'm still holding the car door wide open.

"Hit the top and rang the big fat bell, Angie," Clem says.

I give him a look.

"It's true, Angie. I swear."

"Yes, sweetheart," Mom says. "It's true."

I've imagined this moment so many times. I've pictured myself whooping and laughing when I hear the news. But now that it's really happening, I burst into tears.

Composing on the Fly

I compose my performance piece for the finals all week. A few times, Clem waves his hand in my face to get my attention.

"You're helping me at the time trials, right?" he asks.

"I don't know," I say.

"Angie, I need you."

"I've got to write this poem."

"Do it while you're at the park."

I take a deep breath. "Okay."

Clem smiles. His teeth are the wildest teeth you've ever seen. They poke and dart. Some are thin, some wide, some low, some high. They're like words, each one of them different. I think of Surfer, arrogant and threatening. How different Clem is from him.

"You're awesome," I blurt.

"Thanks," Clem says. He looks at me for a moment, then nods and says, "You too."

It's nice to be on the track again. It feels great to push down with my legs and pedal hard and to feel my stomach lift when I catch air. I offer Clem tips about the track, but he doesn't really need them. He just wants me there. I watch him fly and jump and twist and land hard, solidly, and the whole time, I'm running words through my head, letting them jump and twist and land hard too. That's a cool thing about writing. It takes me all sorts of places, but *I* can take *it* anywhere I go. I can do it anywhere, anytime.

I found this magazine in the library called *the Claremont Review*. It publishes poems and stories by anyone under eighteen. I'm going to send some of my stories to the editors. I've decided that I want to write all my life, no matter what happens. Life changes—it always will change, Mom says. For me, writing just might be the ultimate through-line. Slam Night got me through the last few months. It let me imagine some-thing beyond how uncomfortable we were, how much I missed Dad and how worried I was about Mom. It gave me *a way* to think about all that stuff—a way in and a way out. A way through.

Clem takes second place, which gets him into next week's finals.

"I always knew I had two champions," Mom says once we're back in the car.

"You don't—not yet," Clem tells her.

"You're wrong," Mom says. "We've have hard circumstances the last few months. But you two have managed to come out ahead. "

Mom starts up the Skylark. "Check the map," she tells Clem.

Just like that, we're on our way to see our new home.

A woman with a clipboard gives us a tour of the three-story, three-bedroom townhouse. It's a little tight and there's no yard, but it's *our* house! It's got a fridge and a bathtub and *big* windows. Closets! Drawers! A living room, a dining alcove, a hallway long enough to lie down in. There's even a parking spot for the car.

There's more good news on this bright spring day. After our tour of the house, we stop in at the library.

"Did you get a letter from Dad?" Clem asks as we gaze into the computers.

"Looks like it."

"Did you read it?"

"Not yet."
"Read it."

Angel,

I'm coming home. Mom and I have been Talking about it.

i have made a name for myself here. There was even a news article about my brick work. I joked once with mom that one of us needed to make some trouble. Well Ive been making trouble with my bricks. The article called it art.

That got me jobs in the rich part of town. Now I've got work in Victoria.

Mom tells me you've been making trouble too. Poetry. She says you are winning prizes. Im not surprised my girl. I'll be there in a week. I love you. We will live together in that big house hey?

I love you. I told you that already. I know.

I love you.
Dad

"Three more days, and we're in the townhouse," Clem says. "For the first week, all I'm going to do is cook and eat."

I laugh. And maybe because I know we've got a home to go to, with a fridge and a stove, I'm able to look at Clem straight on, eyes fully open, for the first time in months. The guy is bony. He needs some solid rest and square meals. Come to think of it, I probably do too.

I drag Clem to finals one hour early. I have to be first on the list. I've got to get to the mic before Surfer does. I know he's planning to slur me onstage, announce that I live in a car, make out that I'm pathetic.

Twig introduces me as the "newest, youngest slam champ on the block."

"Go, Angie!" people shout. Even Mercy Girl. I wait until the audience quiets, and then I introduce my poem.

"Things got hard for my family this last year." I say. "Mom lost a bunch of jobs, Dad couldn't find work, and finally we got kicked out of our apartment. My mom, brother and I have been living in a car for the past few months. Some people think this is something to be ashamed of. Anyway, everything's okay now. We just got a home. Subsidized housing. A palace."

People clap and cheer. Some look toward Clem, who looks freaked out. But he manages to give me a thumbs-up.

"What happened, basically, is my family wobbled. That's what we did. But everything wobbles, the Earth in its orbit and a skylark on the wind. How else do you get back to the truth?"

I wait a second, then start sing-hollering my latest performance piece.

Skylark

The street is a vein, a seam, a stain
between you and me, the street
is an asphalt river. I took a long
    swim there.
With my mother and my brother.
We would not let each other drown.
No. We let each other swim there.
No coins in our pockets to weigh us
    down
and our lungs and hearts filled with
hope. And when hope failed, with faith
that the street would do what it was
    meant to do,
deliver us whole and untroubled,
    somewhere new.

Let me start at the beginning.
    We were living
in the Buick Skylark and Mom still
    managed to look
like a million bucks every day...

I don't care whether people clap when I am through. I don't care if I win the finals or not. All I care about is that I've found home.

Acknowledgments

Thank you, John, Anne, Catherine, Meg, and Donald, my siblings and father, with whom I thrived in many houses— you have always been tremendously encouraging. I am very thankful, too, to the poets I met during the years I was between houses, especially the late poets Karl Wendt and Patrick O'Connell. Thank you, Alden, Ezra, and Hazel, with whom I share a home and my heart. Thank you to Scott, Max, Sophia, Ethan, Jess, and Austin—my cup overfilleth! And thanks, Graham Cournoyer, whose Auto Trader ad read like Dadaist poetry and who let me spend a few hours with his 1982 Buick Skylark while writing this book. Finally, thanks to Andrew Wooldridge, my sharp and generous editor.

Sara Cassidy has lived in a logging camp, a five-by-seven-foot survival shelter in the Manitoba bush, a refugee camp (as an international witness), an apartment over a downtown biker bar, in youth hostels in Canada and Scotland as well as in large, comfortable houses. In every place, she had a pen and a journal to help steer her way through. *Skylark* is her fifth book for youth.